HELEN CRESSWELL

A GAME OF CATCH

Illustrated by Ati Forberg

MACMILLAN PUBLISHING CO., INC.
New York

Macmillan Publishing Co., Inc.
866 Third Avenue, New York, N.Y. 10022
First American edition, 1977
Printed in the United States of America
10 9 8 7 6 5 4 3 2 1

LIBRARY OF CONGRESS CATALOGING IN PUBLICATION DATA

Cresswell, Helen.
  A game of catch.

  SUMMARY: A contemporary girl plays a "game of catch"
with two children from an eighteenth-century painting.
  [1. Space and time—Fiction]   I. Forberg, Ati.   II. Title.
PZ7.C8645Gam3   [Fic]   76-46991
ISBN 0-02-725440-2

For Nancy Rowe, with love

1947901

ONE

"Isn't it deep and *dangerous*!" Kate bent over the parapet to peer at the moat below. "And the smell!"

She sniffed in the strong, dark-green smell of moat and stone, remembering piers and seaweed. Hugh followed suit and their gasps made white smoke about them in the frosty air.

"One day we'll bring a rope and scale the walls," Hugh said.

"Someone'd see us and stop us," Kate said, hopeful.

"It's winter. Tour buses don't visit museums in winter."

"There's the caretaker."

"Let's find him." Hugh swung down from the wall. "He'll

1

be old and hoary. Far too hoary to notice us. We'll get him to let us in and have a look round."

"But we hate museums," Kate pointed out.

"Usually, yes. This is different."

He tilted back his head and stared up at the great stone ramparts rearing to the blank winter sky. Suddenly he could feel echoes all around him and shouted "Oy!" and heard *oy . . . oy . . . oy* dying back into the cold stone.

"That made me jump," Kate said.

"Try it."

"Hello!" *Hello . . . lo . . . lo. . . .* The syllables rang in the bitter air. A storm of rooks was roused overhead. They fell out of the sky like great black gloves. Involuntarily Kate put up her arm as a shield but they caught themselves in flight and lifted back up, yelling hoarsely and starting their own echoes.

"I'm Kate!" *Kate . . . Kate . . . .*

"I'm Hugh!" *Hoo . . . hoo . . . hoo . . . .*

"Hello!" *Hello . . . lo . . . lo . . . .* "I'm Kate!" *Kate . . . Kate . . . .*

They were seized with excitement; the whole bare place was suddenly peopled for them.

"What's all the noise?"

They were bemused by the volleys of echoes, and a strange human voice, close at hand, took them by surprise. Besides, they weren't looking. They had their heads tilted back to the battlements and the sky.

"Oh!" Kate said. "Good morning."

"Morning."

"I hope we weren't making too much noise," said Hugh, who always knew how to be polite enough to get himself out of trouble. "We didn't know anyone was about."

"I don't mind a bit of noise myself," said the man. "Not ordinary noise. But echoes is best left be."

They stared at him. "Best left be?" repeated Kate.

"Echoes is funny things. Best left where they belong. Particular in an old place like this. I don't believe in rousing up echoes, myself."

Kate shivered and pulled up her scarf around her throat.

"I expect you'll be the caretaker, sir," said Hugh, keeping up the politeness—even overdoing it a little, Kate thought.

"Joe Whittaker, caretaker," he replied. "One man with a castle to keep singlehanded."

"It must be very hard work," said Hugh.

The caretaker said nothing.

"We thought we'd like to have a look round inside, if it's no trouble," Hugh went on. "We're staying down in the village, and our aunt said we ought to look round the museum. She said it was very interesting."

"Oh, it's that, right enough. They come in busloads like swarms of blessed wasps in the summer."

Kate, picturing a busload of wasps, almost giggled. The echoes had left her feeling like giggling. Instead she said, "I expect you know our Aunt Grace. Her name's Miss Fairley and she lives at the White House."

"Aye," he agreed, "I know Miss Fairley, right enough. And this place is open all days and all weathers, if you don't count Christmas. Open to the public ten till five, admission ten pence and half-price children."

He turned and led the way over the flags to the great studded gate. They followed him, exchanging eyebrows. Cut into one of the doors was another, smaller opening, and they passed through this into the courtyard. It was cold as a cell, a cellar, the high walls cutting out all but a

square of sky. Grass grew between the cracks of the paving stones and Kate, shivering again, half longed for a tour group to break the thin, ringing silence.

The caretaker halted by an arched doorway.

"Main entrance," he said. "I'll get your tickets."

They followed him into a different silence and a different cold. A tiny room, lit by a bare electric light bulb, led off from the hallway. This was evidently the office, for he was busy unlocking drawers and rattling cash boxes.

They waited in the doorway. The room was quite cosy, as much a living room as an office. Coconut matting covered the flags and two paraffin heaters threw little red ruffs of light about them that at least looked warm. There was an old wooden rocking chair, a wireless, and a sink with a shelf of crockery and a half-silvered mirror above it. In one corner was a small stove and kettle and near it an oil-cloth-covered table. The shelves against the far wall were stacked with newspapers and magazines and what looked like boxes of jigsaws.

"Oh! You like jigsaws!" cried Kate.

She was a champion herself, with nearly a hundred in her cupboard and a subscription to a club promised for her birthday.

"Aye."

The caretaker had the tickets ready now, and Hugh handed him the money. "They make the evenings go, do jigsaws."

"I'll send you some of mine, when I get home," Kate promised. The moment she had said it she was surprised at herself. But she had had a sudden picture of the little room at night, one electric light bulb in a great stone well of dark and silence.

"Would you, miss?" His anonymous caretaker's face began to break up now. His eyes began to see them, really see them as people, instead of just two half-price tickets.

"Of course. I've got plenty that I've finished with."

"I'd be grateful, and that's the truth. I *like* a puzzle I've

5

done before—it comes halfway to meet you, so to speak. But a new one—well, it's a real treat, miss, as you'll know yourself."

Kate did. She knew exactly what he meant. There was nothing quite to match the moment when you sat at the table, tipped a brand-new puzzle out of its box and began turning the pieces the right way up. She smiled at him and he smiled back for a moment before his caretaker's face came shuttering down again.

"You'll want to go up them stairs"—he pointed to the far end of the hall—"and turn left. After that, just keep going and in the end you'll come out again at the other side of the stairway. Go in a circle round the square, so to speak. There's arrows, anyhow. You can't go wrong."

"Thank you. We'll go and have a look. Come on, Kate."

They walked down the hall, up the stairs, took a last look at Joe Whittaker's figure outlined against the dim light of his doorway, and went left.

TWO

They were in a wide, long gallery. To the right were tall slit windows, set deeply into the wall. On the other side were doors leading off.

A worn runner of red carpet ran like a road before them. They trod it because the sound of their footsteps on the stone made them feel like intruders. Hugh's fingers closed over the tickets in his pocket. After all, they had paid their money. At the first door they stopped. It was closed.

"Are we meant to go in?" Kate whispered. "It might be private."

"If it was, there'd be a notice."

They stepped off the carpet and tiptoed to the door. Hugh lifted the heavy iron handle and turned it. The door swung slowly open.

"But it's empty!" cried Kate. There was nothing to see but stone walls, stone floor, a large mullioned window and beyond it walls again at the other side of the courtyard. The windows might as well have been of looking glass, offering no view, reflecting only stone.

"We'll try the next one," said Hugh.

They closed the door behind them and walked slowly up the gallery, politely meeting the stares of the bearded men and plump, bare-shouldered ladies. They looked at them out of habit, feeling it was expected of them. They looked at everything—the pieces of tattered tapestry, the crossed pikes, the pottery in glass cases—as if they were on a school outing and supposed to be learning something.

The next room was full of life-size models in glass cases wearing shabby, jewel-encrusted robes. They stared silently at them for a minute and then were back in the gallery, trudging toward the next door. This time it was pictures— etchings of the castle, views of the battlements among the trees, the courtyard swarming with soldiers. Doggedly they followed the red carpet.

By the time they reached the end of the gallery, where it took a right-angled turn to the left, Kate was beginning to feel the old museum-feeling stealing over her. It was a boredom so enormous that it hurt. It was a feeling that if she had to go on looking at dull things with an interested expression on her face for a moment longer she would either go mad or begin to break things. They turned the corner. There before them lay another gallery, another strip of red carpet, another row of blank doorways.

"Oh, *Hugh!*"

"What's the matter?"

"It's horrible, you know it is. Just like all museums. There are three more of these galleries to get through yet. Let's go back."

"No," said Hugh.

"*Please.*"

"No. Look!" He pointed. The door of the first room stood open. Beyond it they could see steps rising up as if through the very ceiling. "That'll be to the battlements."

Kate's eye fell on a notice and a black arrow.

"It is! There's a notice: *To the battlements.*"

Throwing their echoes to the winds, running now and even shouting, they raced to the stairs.

"We can go right round the castle up on top!" cried Hugh.

"We'll be able to see for miles!" cried Kate.

The stairs spiraled up, and they reached a heavy studded door. Hugh gave it a push, and the next minute fresh air was on their faces and they were out in the welcome frost and among the scolding rooks, right on the very roof of the world, it seemed. They ran to the outer edge of the battlement and found that they could just see over the top at the lowest parts, though Kate had to stretch a little to manage it.

"Oh!" she gasped. "Isn't it high!"

The moat that had seemed so deep and dangerous an hour ago lay far and away below, no more than a dyke. Beyond were the stubbled brown fields powdered with frost, the dull pewter of the lake, the broomstick trees.

"There's the church," said Hugh.

"And there's the White House. We're miles above everything. Let's go right round. Let's look from the other side."

They ran to find a new view from the far side, stopping now and then to peer between the cut-out edges of the ramparts.

"I'm actually hot!" Kate gasped when at last they had gone the four sides of the square and were back to the staircase.

"We haven't looked over the other side," said Hugh.

There was a level wall, and they peered over it down into the deep well of the courtyard.

"Hello!" *lo . . . lo . . . .* "I'm Kate!" *Kate . . . Kate . . . .*

The echoes rang like bells; they seemed to strike out of the very stones and spin freely in the upper air. And with them there came again the excitement, the strong feeling that the place was suddenly peopled and alive. They both felt it, and Kate suddenly touched Hugh's arm and cried, "Catch! You're on!" and sped toward the studded door.

She spun giddily down the steps and heard the clatter of Hugh's footsteps following. Out into the wide gallery she sped and heard Hugh's voice following her—"Kate, Kate!"—and the echoes of her name running around her. Then among the echoes she thought she heard another voice saying her name, close at hand. So she ran faster,

11

and heard too the laughter of children, near and clear. But the laughter had no echoes, it simply faded, went swiftly away as if into a great distance.

"Catch me! Catch me!" she cried. But the excitement had gone with the crowding laughter. As she stood still, straining her ears, Hugh was touching her arm and shouting, "Catch! You're on!"

"Hugh! Wait! Hugh!"

But he was away, racing up the gallery under its cold, shafting light. And Kate, without the least desire to catch him, ran after him.

THREE

Mr. Whittaker was still in his office when they reached the entrance hall again. He was seated at the oilcloth-covered table, his hands cupping a steaming mug of tea. He looked up.

"Finished?" he asked.

"We've seen what we want to, thank you," said Hugh truthfully. They had seen one gallery and played catch through the other three.

"Is that all?" asked Kate. "I mean, isn't there a downstairs?" She could have bitten off her tongue. As there was an upstairs, there *had* to be a downstairs. There could be another slice of that endless square to trudge, and she was out of breath and tired of playing catch.

"Stables, mostly. That and storerooms. There's just the one room, over yonder." He nodded his head and they turned to look.

"Sort of banquet hall. Go on, have a look."

They crossed the hall and turned the knob of one side of the great double doors.

"Oh!" said Kate softly. "A real room!"

The door swung to behind them and they advanced a few paces, looking about them. They were in a hall rather than a room, with long mullioned windows running down to the floor on one side. On the other sides a carved wooden gallery ran, with flags and banners hanging from poles at intervals. A refectory table stood in the middle with twenty or more chairs set around it. On the walls hung the usual tapestries, the usual portraits. There was certainly nothing homelike about it. And yet the room was not hushed as the others had been; the air was less cold.

"It might only have been yesterday," said Kate to herself.

"What might?" asked Hugh. He was wandering over by the great stone fireplace, and for a moment found himself putting out his hands as if to warm them at a blaze.

Hastily he pulled them back and put them in his pockets, taking a quick look to see if Kate were watching. She was.

"It *is* warmer in here," she said.

"Probably something to do with it being on the ground floor," he replied. "Not so high up, and all that." It sounded lame, even to him.

"No. It's nothing to do with that at all. Hugh, did *you* hear the voices?"

"What voices?" He threw himself down in a padded chair, his legs stretched out in front of him.

"Up in the gallery, just after we came down from the roof. Voices calling my name, and then children laughing. Didn't you hear?"

"It was me calling, idiot," he said.

"And someone else."

"Echoes."

"There *were* echoes," she agreed. "But these were real. At least, not exactly real, because they didn't have echoes."

"What *are* you talking about?" he said.

"I told you. You did hear them. You must have. Didn't you?"

For a moment he did not reply.

"Yes, I did," he said at last. "I was testing you."

"Thank you very much."

"You know what I mean. You're always imagining things."

"Not this," she said.

For a while neither of them said anything. Even the silence was ordinary now, just any silence in any room.

"It's something to do with the echoes," said Kate. "As if in calling and making them answer we were making something else answer too. Some*one* else."

"So we'll ask old Whittaker," Hugh said. "He said something about the echoes when we first saw him."

" 'Echoes is best left be.' "

"That's it. You see? He'll know what's going on."

He got up.

"But, Hugh, wait a minute."

He turned.

"Do you think we should? We don't want to spoil it. Perhaps telling might spoil it for them."

"Them?"

"Whoever they are. The children. They seemed so happy and excited. They were laughing."

"Look, if there's anyone here, he'll know about it. He lives here. Telling him won't make any difference."

"I suppose not."

They went back across the entrance hall and stood in the doorway of the caretaker's room waiting for him to notice them.

He did not look up, but he evidently knew they were there.

"Seen everything, then?"

"Yes, thank you."

"We liked that room," Kate told him. "It seemed—lived in."

He did look up then, but said nothing, merely looking hard at their faces as if trying to read something there.

"Staying here long?" he asked.

"Only three more days," Hugh replied. "We're just staying while our parents finish tidying things up. We've sold our house."

"We're going abroad to Canada," Kate said. "For five years."

"Not that we particularly want to," added Hugh.

The caretaker was silent. Kate could feel the situation slipping away and with sudden inspiration said, "I've just thought, I'd better bring those jigsaws up to you. Most of them have been packed, but I've got some with me. You can have those."

17

"You make sure you want to part with them first. An old jigsaw is an old friend. *I* know that."

"Oh, I'm sure," she lied. "I'll bring them tomorrow."

"It must be lonely here, Mr. Whittaker," said Hugh.

"It don't matter how much you're alone if you don't feel alone," he replied.

"I don't think I'd feel alone here, either," Kate said.

He looked sharply at her, and she met his gaze.

"I heard someone calling my name, up in the galleries," she said. "And children, laughing."

He seemed to let out a long-held breath.

"Did you, now?" he said at last.

"And everything came alive, as if the whole place was suddenly crowded. It was after we'd been on the battlements making echoes."

"Ah, echoes. It'd be the echoes you heard."

"No," put in Hugh, "they called Kate's name. I heard them as well."

"Kate!" replied the old man. "You're called Kate, are you? It's the name!"

For a minute nobody spoke, then Hugh boldly said, "You do know what we're talking about, don't you?"

"Oh, yes," he agreed slowly. "I know, right enough. Here, look."

He got up and came out into the hall. Silently he pointed behind them and they turned and saw a picture. It showed two children, a girl and a boy of about their own ages. The girl wore a long, apple-green dress tied with a sash of dark olive. She was laughing and stretching out her hands to catch the ball that the boy was holding up as if to tease her. He was all in brown, trimmed with lace at the neck

18

and cuffs, and his dark hair curled to his shoulders. He, too, was laughing.

Hugh, moving closer, read out the inscription set into the wide gilt frame.

"The Lady Katherine Cottam and her brother, Charles, painted by the local artist, James Hammond. Their father, Lord Cecil Cottam, was the last resident of Bottrel Castle, and left in 1790 for the family seat in Cumberland, where the Cottam family still live."

"But they didn't really leave at all," said Kate then. "They're still here."

The caretaker nodded.

"It's the name, isn't it?" she went on. "We're both called Katherine."

"And we kept calling our names to start the echoes," added Hugh.

"Things latch themselves on to names. Names mean more than most people suppose. And echoes can only give back what you give 'em. You got to give an echo the right name."

Footsteps sounded in the courtyard and the door was pushed open. They swung around.

"Customers," said the caretaker, and went back to his office.

"We'll come again tomorrow," Kate called after him. They went past the three ladies delving in their purses for coins, and on into the cold stone well of the courtyard. They walked in silence through the main gates, over the ramparts and across the drawbridge. Neither of them spoke until they were on the path toward home over the meadows, where there were no echoes.

FOUR

That night it froze. It was not a hard black frost that merely took the sky and trees from the lake and darkened the puddles in the ruts. It stole reflections but it brought its own, too. It had come combing softly down in the night through the bare trees and been caught among their boughs in straws. It was like salt on the stubble.

Kate and Hugh went out to test the ice on the lake, the castle forgotten in the huge excitement of the frost. They left their skates behind, afraid of taking too much for granted.

Now they stood in the stiffly furred grasses by the water's edge and banged the ice with their heels, delighted that they could not break it. Hugh found a stick and hammered, but the stick broke.

"It might be all right," he said.

"In another day, Aunt Grace said. She said leave it another day."

They were alone in that white, silent landscape, and the thought of a sudden dark hole in the ice was terrifying.

"We'll come down again after dinner and bring a hammer," he said. "We can't tell for sure like this."

"We've got to come back again, anyway," said Kate. "I told Mr. Whittaker I'd bring those puzzles."

"You and your castle," he scoffed. "You and your old echoes."

"They're no more mine than yours!" cried Kate defensively. "You were there, too. I thought you said you heard them."

"I might have *thought* so, at the time. But not now."

She stared at him, dismayed.

"But it was real," she cried. "You know it was. And the picture! And Mr. Whittaker! He knew it was real."

"Look," he said, "when people live on their own, they start imagining things. It's only natural, if you think about it. Day after day in that great old place with nothing to do but jigsaws and hardly a customer a week in the winter."

"The trouble with you is that you never want to believe anything," said Kate. "Even when it's right under your nose you don't want to believe in it."

"I've just got common sense, that's all. If you think for a minute, the whole thing's impossible, Kate. There's two hundred years between them and us. And all the echoes in the world can't bridge *that*."

"They can, they can!" insisted Kate. "And nothing's impossible!" But she said it to herself.

"We'll go and make that slide in the drive," said Hugh. He gave the ice a final thwack with the stick and hared off over the crunching turf.

After dinner they took a hammer and went to the lake again.

"Better give it another day, I suppose," said Hugh reluctantly. "So we may as well go up to your castle."

They hid their skates under a bush and set off, Kate with a large parcel under her arm. But the visit was a disappointing one. Yesterday they had been caught unawares; there had been the sheer magic of surprise. But today the echoes were locked in by more than just the frost, and

22

though Kate longed to stand and call her name out of the stones, she could not.

It was not only that Hugh was there beside her, unbelieving now and half ready to mock; it was that she felt quite certain that the whole thing was not so simple as it seemed. It was not just a matter of calling up echoes as if they alone were the key to a secret lock. There was something else besides. And she knew, quite certainly, that she could shout her name a thousand times today without the least stir from the stone. The centuries had settled back into place again.

Even the caretaker seemed aware of it. He thanked her for the jigsaws, unwrapping the parcel eagerly and stacking the boxes neatly on his shelves along with the others.

"That'll take care of a good few hours," he said with satisfaction.

But he said nothing about their conversation of the day before. He was in a talkative mood. Hugh asked him what he thought about the ice on the lake, and he launched into stories of his own childhood and the winters he could remember, with snow high as barn doors and ice you could light fires on. Hugh and Kate listened, fascinated—until, when at last they walked away over the drawbridge, the whole landscape seemed to have shrunk since they last saw it. They walked rapidly home, thinking of a hot fire, tea and television, tired of frost.

Next morning they had to go into the nearby town to shop. Their aunt wanted to buy them clothes for Canada.

"We can buy things over there," Kate protested. "There are shops, aren't there?"

"There's nowhere like England for woolies," replied their aunt. "And you'll need plenty of those where you're going."

23

And so there was only an hour of daylight left when at last they reached the lake. Hurriedly they pulled up the laces on their boots, delighted to find that no one had been before them. There was not a scar, not a mark on the whole wide sweep of it, and it beckoned them with the perfection of untrodden snow.

Hugh was the first on, with a few swift, thrusting strokes, and by the time Kate had tied her last lace he was already in the distance, making straight across the middle to the far side.

Kate looked about her at the flawless ice and followed him, her eyes fixed on the furrows left by his blades. But as her fear of the tracklessness vanished, she too was ranging the whole lake, like a bird with the whole vast air of

the sky to choose from. Once, years ago, she could remember skating on a frozen canal, sweeping straight up a long white endless road between the stiff sedges until darkness fell. But she had never before been let loose in a freedom like this, with infinite possible paths spoking about her, endless choice. It was almost too much, like a new dimension.

"Kate! Kate!" She heard Hugh calling and turned to see that he too was skating in great arcs, greedily, as if trying to print his signature over the whole blank page of the lake. He beckoned, but she would not go to him, and sped into new distances, staking her own claim.

As the afternoon wore on they hardly met or even came close to each other, spellbound in their private mazes.

But the dusk began to gather swiftly, and the sun suddenly appeared at the rim of the meadows, huge and orange in a sky surprisingly tender and tinged with green.

"Kate! Kate!" Hugh was calling again from the far side of the lake. "Catch me! Kate!"

And in that moment the frost released its echoes and she heard her name go folding away across the darkening meadows— *Kate . . . Kate . . . Kate . . .* —and on into silence.

"Kate! Kate!" She checked, turned, and drove fast toward him. "Catch me!" *Catch . . . catch . . . .* Then again her name, nearer now, "Kate, Kate!" without echoes, and the sound of steel blades tearing the ice.

Slowing, she looked over to her right, and saw, impossibly, furrows moving across the ice, turning, wheeling, curving like smoke tracks in the sky. Forgetting Hugh, she veered to follow, but always they were beyond her, furling out of the ice ahead, curving mischievously aside, doubling back, elusive as smoke.

"Kate! Kate!" She no longer knew who was calling her, nor cared. Intent on the beckoning tracks she sped and thought she heard laughter beyond the hissing of her own skates and the pounding in her ears.

"Kate!" It *was* Hugh's voice now, close by, and she lifted her eyes to look at him, a stranger for a moment after the spellbound hour when only their paths had crossed.

"You're not even trying to catch me!" he cried. "What are you playing at? Kate!"

But she was away again, panic-stricken now because she had lost track of the unreeling thread and was left with a maze of thin lines, crossing and recrossing endlessly. She stopped and looked about her, listening for the sharp scything of blades that would betray her quarry. There

26

was nothing. She strained her eyes into the dusk and could just make out her brother's figure away again at the far end of the lake. The sun had dropped. It was impossible to unravel the skein on the ice. Everything had gone away into darkness and silence.

She skated to where Hugh was already on the bank changing his boots. He did not look up. If she was ever to tell him what had happened now was the time, with the frost falling, the cold translating into whiteness and anything possible after the long spell on ice.

But with her first steps onto the bank the world seemed to dip and then steady again, as it did after a day at sea. Her head spun; she sat down fumbling with her laces, and felt the delicious cold of the hoar against her hot legs.

"I forgot my gloves," Hugh said. "I shall get hot-aches when we get in."

"Serve you right," she heard herself say. Served him right for what? She hardly knew. But the moment had passed, and she said no more. They went home between the dark hedges of the lane which was all metal now, silver and iron.

"Another frost tonight," said Hugh. Kate smiled.

FIVE

It did freeze again. It was as if everything were conspiring with the echoes, ground and water turning to stone, the air thin and bitter. Kate woke to see it and knew that she must spend the day seeking. In particular she knew that she must go to the castle alone.

It was easy to get away that morning. Hugh had heard that there was a canal beyond the village, and intended to skate along it right into the next village.

"I don't feel like skating again," Kate said when he told her.

"Come on," he urged. "Aunt Grace says it's a snow sky today. If it snows you won't get another chance."

"I don't want to, Hugh. Honestly."

"I know where you'll go," he told her. "Up to your old castle."

"I might."

She waited until he had left and then set out up the lane toward the castle. There was a mist as well as the frost, and at first she could not see even the castle's outline, in a curiously shrunken world, a world with walls now.

As she walked it seemed as if everything about her contained a secret from which she alone was shut out. Even the cattle, kneeling in the frosty grass, turned their heads to stare after her curiously as she passed, slowly blowing out their white breath.

All the time she was asking herself questions.

"Is it the picture on the wall that matters? If the picture was taken away, would they go with it?"

She did not know the answer.

"Yesterday, on the lake, whose time was it, theirs or ours? Had they come forward to meet us, or were Hugh and I skating two hundred years ago?"

There was no answer to this either. The frost and the ice and the landscape were all anonymous. Yesterday might have been any day taken from all time. It might have been yesterday or it might have been a thousand years ago.

She looked about her and realized that the same was true today. The mist had swallowed the village behind her. She saw not a single landmark of time, only the fields, the sky and the weather. She hurried her steps toward the castle and Joe Whittaker, who stood with his feet firmly planted in the twentieth century and could anchor her safely there, too.

As she went under the high archway into the center courtyard she could see his light bulb burning through the dusty window. She tiptoed into the hallway, not wanting him to know that she was there yet. She gazed up at the picture, looking for clues. But the children were not even looking at her, they were looking at each other, intent on their game and the ball in the boy's hand. There was only one clue, and even that was hardly more than a hint.

"They're wearing warm clothes—velvet and wool," she thought. "And the girl has a muff hanging from her wrist. It was winter. It could have been this very time of year."

If the girl had been wearing muslin and a straw hat, at least Kate would have known the answer to one of her questions. At least she would have known that yesterday on the frozen lake it had not been Hugh and herself who had stepped out of their time and into that of the picture.

"It's you again, is it, miss?"

She found Joe Whittaker at her elbow, muffler tucked in his jacket, steaming mug of tea in hand.

"Oh! You made me jump. Yes. I wanted to look at the picture again." They stared up at it together.

"It *is* a mystery," remarked the caretaker at last. "No doubt about it. Even to me, and I live with it."

Kate said nothing.

"Have a cup of tea," he invited. "I've only just mashed."

She followed him into the office and sat in the rocking chair near the oil stove. She hugged her knees and watched him busy with the crockery, waiting for the right moment to tell her story. The opening came easily, as it happened.

"You put trust in the ice yesterday, then," he said. "I saw you away down there from up top. Good little pair of skaters you are."

"Did you watch long?" she asked quickly. "What time was it?"

"Time? I can't say. I don't reckon much by the clock myself. Near dusk, I suppose."

She bent forward.

"Did you—I don't suppose you saw the others, too?"

"Others, miss?" He came over with a cup and saucer and set it down on the table beside her.

"Yes, the other two. There were four of us—in the end, at any rate."

He shook his head.

"I didn't see no four of you. Must've been after."

"Must've been," she agreed. After all, why should he

31

have seen them? Even she had seen only the unfurling of their tracks. But she had half hoped that the caretaker, who lived with echoes and knew that time had nothing to do with clocks, might have taken the centuries in his stride.

"What I suppose is," he went on surprisingly, "that your friends weren't there to *be* seen."

"But they were!" she cried. "I heard them!"

"Oh they were there, right enough," he agreed. "No one knows that better than me. But not to be *seen*."

"I saw their marks on the ice. I heard them. Do you think I'll ever actually see them? Do you?"

"Depends how much you want to, I suppose."

"Oh, I *really* want to, Mr. Whittaker. Just for a moment, even. I want to believe in them."

"Seeing is believing," he said. "We've always to see before we'll believe."

"I don't think Hugh would believe even if he *saw*," she said. "That's really why I want to see them so badly. It always seems to be Hugh that's right and me that's wrong. I'm not saying anything against him, mind, it's just that we're different. Everyone says we are. But I was so sure about this, and at first I thought Hugh was as well. But now he's gone all sensible, as usual, and says I'm imagining things."

"So far as *I* know," said Joe Whittaker slowly, as if airing an opinion to which he had given a great deal of thought, "there ain't all that much difference between seeing and imagining. In the end you might say the two was one and the same thing."

"You mean that if a thing *feels* real, it is?"

"Something like that," he said.

32

Kate drank her tea and stared at him over the top of her cup. There was something she meant to ask him, something that was at the very tip of her tongue but she couldn't quite remember. He too sat sipping his tea, and just then the electric light suddenly paled as a shaft of sunlight flooded the little room.

"The sun's out!" Kate cried. "And I wanted to skate again! We go tomorrow. If I don't see them today, I never shall!"

"Gone for five years you'll be, you say?"

"Yes. But I'll tell you this. If I don't see them, I'll come back. The minute we get back from Canada I'll come straight down here and . . . ."

She broke off. He was shaking his head.

"You'll be five years older," he said.

"What of it?"

"And they won't."

Suddenly she saw what he meant. *Their* time was standing still, but hers was still moving. She was not playing an endless game of ball in a gilt frame and waiting for an echo to bring her back to life. She stood up. "I'll have to be going."

He went with her into the hall and suddenly she remembered the question she had been going to ask him.

"What did you mean when you said you knew they were down there, Mr. Whittaker? You said, 'Nobody knows it better than me.' What did you mean, please?"

He looked up at the picture and that, too, was bathed in sunshine now, kindling the dark oils, bringing the two children forward out of their dark background.

"I knew by that," he said.

She stared at him. She half thought she knew what he was going to tell her, but it seemed impossible.

He jerked his head toward the picture.

"They'd gone."

Now that he had actually said it, it was still impossible.

"So you see, miss, you were right. And that brother of yours was wrong."

So they said their good-bys and the caretaker went back to his little room and got out the sweeping brushes, because the sun had lit up the corners and more dust than even he could bear. As for Kate, she walked home with a head full of questions again, because in the puzzle she was trying to solve, every answer brought a new question with it. It was like trying to do a jigsaw with half the pieces missing.

SIX

The sun stayed out for an hour or two and then suddenly went in. The sky filled, a soft, gray snow sky.

"We might be able to skate, if we hurry," Kate said after dinner. "The snow might not come for hours, yet. It might not even come at all."

"It'll come, all right," said their aunt. "It'll come thick and heavy. You get down to the lake, if that's what you want. Though you'll be getting all the skating you want over there."

"Not this kind of skating," thought Kate.

As they went up the now familiar lane she was filled with unbearable excitement. It seemed certain to her now that today time would finally run free and unfetter all the echoes and the unseen voices.

When they reached the lake they saw that the sun had wiped the slate of the ice clean, and it was brand new again. And this time it was Kate who was away first, making a beeline for the far side. She heard Hugh's voice, "Kate, wait! Kate!"

She skated on, pretending not to have heard. She wanted Hugh to make his own tracks, to leave her alone. She wanted to make the same patterns as yesterday's all over again, history to repeat itself. She was making toward the moment just before dusk when the invisible blades would

35

come scything out of nowhere and the game of catch would begin again.

But things went wrong. Hugh had been skating all morning, had followed the frozen canal to Withenshaw and back alone, and was tired of the sound of his own skates and the endless white of ice. He started to follow.

"Look out! I'm coming!"

She checked and looked back over her shoulder to see him coming after her with long, swift strokes, and she cried, "No, I'm not playing! Go away!"

But he came on, so she turned and sped away and found herself playing catch without meaning to at all, the wrong game of catch.

But even this was more than just a game, because if he caught her it would be all up. She would have to chase him, too, and then the whole thing would begin all over again, and the afternoon would waste away. She drove fast along the length of the lake, heading for the tiny, reed-trimmed islands that scattered the ice. She could dodge him there. Hugh was a better skater, and it was her only chance.

He was still a good way behind her when she reached the first island, caught a blade in a tuft that still showed through the ice, and fell. For a moment she lay there, her face pressed against the ice, seeing the crust of hoar on the rush spears that were bent under her.

Then Hugh was standing over her.

"Kate! Are you all right? Can you get up?"

She lifted herself slowly onto her hands and knees, but as soon as she tried to get to her feet she groaned and fell to her knees again.

"My foot hurts," she said. "No, my ankle."

She turned sideways to a sitting position and looked up into his worried face.

"You must have sprained your ankle."

"Not actually sprained it. It just hurts."

"Can you make it to the bank, if I help you?"

She did not reply. She was looking beyond him to the other side of the lake, where a group of figures had just appeared.

"Look!"

He followed her gaze.

"Looks like the Lewises. I can see their sled. Lucky dogs."

So the afternoon was lost, after all. There was no need now to go on pretending about her foot. Whether she played catch or not, whether she skated fast or slowly, it made no difference.

"I'll see if I can get up now," she said.

Hugh held her hands and she got to her feet.

"How does it feel?"

She took a testing step forward.

"All right, I think." Her ankle did hurt a little. She hadn't really been going to pretend it was sprained, just twisted, so that she couldn't play catch with Hugh. He was looking in the other direction again, and they could hear shouts and laughter floating over the ice.

"See if you can make it over to the other side," he said. She could tell that he was impatient, hoping that she wasn't going to spoil things. She skated slowly off, careful not to go too fast, and he came up alongside.

"You must have just given it a twist," he said. "I expect it'll wear off in a bit if you go carefully."

"I'll just go slowly round till it does," she said. "You go over to the others. They're taking turns on the sled, by the look of it."

Three of them were towing long ropes, harnessed like horses. Deborah, the youngest Lewis, was sitting bolt upright on the sled, waving her arms and shouting.

"Sure you'll be all right?" He hesitated.

"Positive."

She watched him skate over to join them, wondering why she didn't go herself now that the lake was crowded and the last hope of a game of catch had gone.

She was gliding dreamily around the circumference of the lake when the snow began to fall. She paused, and stood by the row of pollards, scenting the change, feeling the blotting-out of frost that was almost like warmth. The flakes were large and tissue-thin, they floated like white skeleton leaves, and the thicker they fell the faster they seemed to spin. She blinked as they melted on her hot face and ran into her eyes, and when she moved off again she was giddy with their swirling motion.

She realized that she was just by the fence where they had left their things, and stopped again. There was no sign of the others and she listened for their voices, but there was only the enormous blanketing silence of falling snow. They seemed to have gone right away.

She climbed onto the bank and unlaced her boots. Then she hung them on the fence beside Hugh's boots and overcoat and went again to the rim of the lake, straining her ears and eyes into the dizzy mist of whiteness. And as she stared, she did hear voices, and laughter, very faint and muffled. They seemed to be coming not from the ice, but from behind her, and once, quite clearly, she heard her name being called, "Kate! Kate!"

She began to run, stumbling here and there over roots and tussocks because now the snow was falling so thickly that she could see only a yard or two ahead.

"Kate! Catch! Catch!"

"I'm coming! Wait, I'm coming!" she cried, and although there were no echoes here, even in the muffling snow she knew that her voice was ringing, carrying, crossing centuries.

"Catch!" The voice was close by, and as she strained her eyes into the spinning snow something came flying toward her and fell at her feet with a soft thud.

She stared down. It was a ball.

"So *this* is the real game of catch," she thought, and picked it up.

SEVEN

For a moment she stared down at the ball in her hands. It was quite soft and made of dark red leather, sewn together in segments. Then she looked up and they were there, both of them.

Though they were divided from her by the falling snow she saw them clearly, and they were watching her, too, expectantly. Suddenly the girl stretched out her hands and without thinking Kate tossed the leather ball back straight into her waiting palms. The girl laughed and shook her hair, then darted off.

"Don't go!" she cried. "Kate!" She called the name again. "Kate!"

"Things latch themselves on to names," Joe Whittaker had said.

But the girl had already turned; she threw the ball to the boy, who leaped nimbly forward to catch it before it touched the ground. He straightened up and looked at Kate.

"Catch!" he cried suddenly, and again the ball was in her hands. She threw it back to him and the girl came running from behind the curtain of snow again to catch it in her turn. They tossed it backward and forward, backward

40

and forward, and all the time Kate, watching the ball, watching them, was thinking fast and furiously. And as the ball came to her the next time she held it firmly between both hands and waited. If she kept it, the spell would be broken and they would stay forever. It was the ball in flight that bridged the centuries. Without it they could never return.

They stood waiting, watching her. The girl, puzzled, smiled and held out her hands. Kate shook her head and put the ball behind her back. They waited, all three of them, the game of catch suspended and the snow falling silently all about them.

"Kate! Kate!" Voices were calling in the distance. She saw the girl stiffen, listening. "Where are you? Kate! Kate!"

The voices were nearer; Kate could hear Hugh's among the yells of the Lewises. What would *they* make of the girl in green velvet and the boy with his long hair brushing his shoulders and shirt frilled at his thin wrists? She stared at their white, frightened faces, and hesitated. Then she brought the ball from behind her back and held it up.

The girl's face cleared, she nodded delightedly and ran forward a few paces from her brother, and Kate, smiling back, threw the ball straight into her cupped hands. For an instant the girl stood there and then with a swift wave turned and ran, the boy after her. They swam into blurs in the snowstorm and were gone.

"Kate! Kate! Where are you!"

She began to run, playing a new game of catch. Now she was hunter and hunted together. She kept her eyes down at first, looking for footprints, but there was nothing to guide her but laughter ahead and now and again a glimpse of pale green or brown. The farther she ran the fainter the laughter grew, and as it dwindled for the last time she halted, panting for breath, and found herself right on the drawbridge of the castle.

Through the great stone arch she hurried and across the high courtyard with its strange snow-light and muffled echoes. The caretaker's bulb burned behind his long window, but as she ran into the entrance hall and stopped in front of the picture she saw that the room was empty. Joe Whittaker was making the lonely rounds of his castle, battening it against the snow.

She stared up. They were there ahead of her, posed and careless as if nothing had ever happened. They had stepped back into the gilt frame and another time and now they did not even look at her, absorbed in their private game of catch.

And yet, as she stared, Kate felt that there was something different. The children were the same, their clothes, their faces. Impossible to explain—and yet different. Still the girl held up the ball and the boy waited for her throw.

"Perhaps he'll wait another hundred years," Kate thought. She knew that the game was over for her now. Slowly she turned and went out into the snow. It was falling lightly now, the flakes went drifting dreamily with all the time in the world. Over the drawbridge she went and started across the darkening meadows. Down by the lake she could see the outline of a small figure approaching. It was Hugh, alone. The others had gone home, but he had waited. He had seen her, too, because he waved and she heard him call, "Kate! Kate!"

And in those moments as they ran toward each other she suddenly knew what had been different about the picture. *The girl had been holding the ball!* Surely, *surely,* before it had been she who was stretching out her hands

43

to catch it, while the boy held it aloft, teasing her? She, Kate, had been the last to throw it in that strange, triangular game of catch. And she had thrown it not to the boy, but the girl.

"Kate!" Their paths met. "Where have you been? I've been looking everywhere."

"I lost my way in the snowstorm," was all she said, and they went together through the last gate of the fields and into the lane. And still she was trying to remember how the picture had looked yesterday. Surely it had been the boy who held the ball? And the girl had it now, and would have it for who knew how many years to come. Perhaps forever?

A herd of cows was being driven home along the lane. Kate and Hugh pressed against the hedge and watched them lumber by, bringing a strong, summer hay-smell into the pure air of the frost. Snowflakes settled on their warm leather foreheads and fringed their round brown eyes.

When the cows had passed, the two of them had the lane to themselves again. It gleamed ahead of them in the dusk, showing their tired legs the way home.

"Surely the ball has changed hands," Kate thought again. The snow went on falling.